# Favorite Fairy Tales

## TOLD IN CZECHOSLOVAKIA

D1255441

# Favorite Fairy Tales

## TOLD IN CZECHOSLOVAKIA

Retold by Virginia Haviland

Illustrated by Anca Hariton

*A Beech Tree Paperback Book*  *New York*

First Beech Tree Edition, 1995, published by arrangement with Little, Brown and Co.
Printed in the United States of America

10 9 8 7 6 5 4 3 2 1

*These stories have been retold from the following sources:*

"The Twelve Months" and "The Three Golden Hairs of Grandfather Know All" are retold from *Fairy Tales of the Slav Peasants and Herdsmen,* from the French of Aleksandr Borejko Chodzko; translated and illustrated by Emily J. Harding (London, George Allen, 1896).

"The Wood Fairy" is retold from a literal translation by Halina Berovetz of the story told by Bozena Nemcova in *Babička* (Praha, Státní nakl. dětské knihy,1951) and from the translation by W.W. Strickland of the version by Karel Erben in *Panslavonic Folklore* (New York, B. Westermann, 1930).

"The Shepherd's Nosegay" and "Kuratko the Terrible" are included as told in *The Shoemaker's Apron* by Parker Fillmore (New York, Harcourt, Brace and Company, 1920). Copyright 1920, by Parker Fillmore, copyright 1948, by Louise Fillmore. Reprinted by permission of Harcourt, Brace & World, Inc.

Library of Congress Cataloging-in-Publication Data

Haviland, Virginia, 1911–1988
    Favorite fairy tales told in Czechoslovakia / retold by Virginia Haviland ; illustrated by Anca Hariton.
      p. cm.
    Contents: The twelve months — Kuratko the Terrible — The wood fairy— The shepherd's nosegay — The three golden hairs of Grandfather Know All.
    ISBN 0-688-12593-X (pbk.)
    1. Fairy tales — Czech Republic.   2. Fairy Tales—Slovakia.
  [1. Fairy Tales.     2. Czechs—folklore.     3. Slovaks—Folklore.
  4. Folklore—Czech Republic.   5. Folklore—Slovakia.]    I. Title.
  PZ8.H295Fas  1995
  [398.21'09437]—dc20                   94–1502
                                        CIP
                                        AC

Minor editorial and style changes have been made in the stories for these new editions.

# Contents

The Twelve Months                        7

Kuratko the Terrible                  25

The Wood Fairy                        37

The Shepherd's Nosegay            51

The Three Golden Hairs of        69
Grandfather Know All

# The Twelve Months

# The Twelve Months

THERE WAS ONCE a widow who had a daughter named Holena. In the cottage with them lived Holena's stepsister, Marushka. Now Marushka was so pretty and good that the other two disliked her and made her do all the hard work. She had to sweep the rooms, cook, wash, sew, spin, and weave, and she had to bring in the hay from the meadow and milk the cow. Holena, who was not pretty, did nothing but dress up in her best clothes and amuse herself with one thing after another.

But Marushka never complained. Patiently she bore the scoldings and bad tempers of the mother and daughter. Holena's ugliness increased, while Marushka became even lovelier to look at. This made the other two more tyrannical and grumpy than ever. At length they determined to get rid of her, for they knew that Holena would have no suitors while Marushka was there to be seen.

One day in the middle of winter Holena said she wanted some violets. "Listen!" she cried to Marushka. "You must go up on the mountain and find me some violets. And they must be fresh and sweet-scented. Do you hear?"

"But whoever heard of violets blooming in the snow!" cried Marushka.

"You wretched creature! Do you dare to disobey me? Not another word! Off with you, and don't come back without the violets!"

The stepmother added her threats, and the two pushed Marushka out of the cottage and shut the door behind her.

Marushka, weeping, made her way to the mountain. The snow lay deep, and there was no trace of any other human being. For a long time she wandered hither and thither and became lost in the woods. She was very hungry and shivered with cold. She was almost ready to give up, when she saw a light in the distance. Marushka climbed toward it until she reached the very top of the mountain.

Upon the highest peak she found a large fire burning and twelve men in long white robes sitting around it. Three had white hair, three were not quite so old, three were young and handsome, and the rest still younger. These were the twelve months of the year, and they sat silently looking at the fire, each one on a block of stone. The great January was placed higher than the others. He was older than they, and his hair and beard were white as snow. In his hand he held a wand.

At first Marushka was afraid, but after a while her courage returned. Drawing near, she said, "Good men, may I warm myself at your fire? I am chilled by the winter cold."

The great January raised his head and asked, "What brings you here, my child? What do you seek?"

"I am looking for violets," replied Marushka.

"This is not the season for violets. Do you not see the snow everywhere?"

"Yes," was Marushka's reply, "but my stepmother and my stepsister have ordered me to bring them violets from your mountain. If I return without them, they will kill me. I pray you, good sirs, to tell me where to find them."

The great January arose and went over to one of the youngest of the months. Placing his wand in that month's hand, he said, "Brother March, take the highest place."

March obeyed, at the same time waving his wand over the fire. Immediately the flames rose toward the sky. The snow began to melt, the trees and shrubs to bud. The grass became green, and between the blades peeped the pale primrose. It was spring, and the meadows turned blue with violets.

"Gather them quickly, Marushka," said March.

Joyfully, Marushka hastened to pick the flowers and soon had a large bouquet. She thanked the months and hastened home. Holena and her mother were amazed at the sight of the flowers and at their fragrance, which filled the house.

"Where did you pick them?" asked Holena.

"Under the trees on the mountain," she replied.

Holena took the flowers without thanking Marushka for the trouble she had taken to get them.

The next day Holena called to Marushka again and said, "I long to taste strawberries. Run and fetch me some from the mountain, and see to it that they are sweet and ripe."

"But whoever heard of strawberries ripening in the snow?" said Marushka.

"Hold your tongue! Go after the strawberries and don't come back without them."

Holena's mother also ordered Marushka to gather the berries. They pushed her out of the house and bolted the door behind her.

Unhappily, Marushka made her way to the mountain again and climbed until she came to the fire where the twelve months sat.

"Good men, may I warm myself at your fire? The winter wind chills me."

The great January raised his head and asked, "Why do you come here? What do you seek?"

"I am looking for strawberries," she replied.

"But we are in the midst of winter. Strawberries do not grow in the snow."

"I know," said Marushka sadly, "but my stepmother and stepsister have ordered me to bring them strawberries. I dare not return without them. Pray, good sirs, tell me where to find them."

The great January arose and went over to the month opposite him. Putting his wand into that month's hand, he said, "Brother June, take the highest place."

June obeyed, and as he waved his wand over the fire, the flames leaped toward the sky. Instantly the snow melted, the earth became green with grass and the trees with leaves. Birds began to sing and flowers blossomed in the forest. It was summer, and in the sunny glades star-shaped blooms changed into ripe red strawberries.

"Gather them quickly," said June.

Joyfully, Marushka thanked the months, and when she had filled her apron, ran happily home. The strawberries greatly surprised Holena and her mother. "Wherever did you find them?" asked Holena, crossly.

"Up on the mountain," replied Marushka.

Holena gave a few to her mother and ate the rest herself. Not even one did she offer to Marushka. But on the third day she had tired of strawberries and fancied having some fresh red apples.

"Run, Marushka," she demanded, "and fetch me fresh red apples from the mountain."

"Apples in winter!" exclaimed Marushka. "Why, the trees have neither leaves nor fruit on them now."

"You idle girl! Go this minute, and don't come back unless you bring the apples."

As before, the widow added her commands and threats. The two seized Marushka roughly and turned her out of the house.

Poor Marushka went weeping through deep snow up the mountain till she came again to the fire where the twelve months sat.

"Good men, may I warm myself at your fire?"

The great January raised his head and asked, "Why do you come here? What do you seek?"

"I come to look for red apples," replied Marushka.

"But this is winter and not the season for apples," answered January.

"I know. But my stepmother and her daughter have ordered me to fetch them red apples from the mountain, and I dare not return without them. Pray, good sirs, tell me where to find them."

The great January arose and went to one of the elderly months, to whom he handed his wand.

"Brother September, take the highest place."

September moved to the highest seat, which January had occupied. He waved the wand over the fire, and a flare of red flames made the snow disappear. The trees leafed out, then brightened with autumn colors. A frosty wind began to scatter the leaves through the forest.

Marushka looked about and spied an apple tree on which hung ripe red fruit. She ran and shook the tree. One apple fell and then another. "That is enough," said September. "Now hurry home."

Marushka thanked the months and went down the mountain joyfully.

At home Holena and her mother marveled at the fruit. "Where did you gather these apples?" Holena asked.

"On the mountaintop," answered Marushka.

"Why did you not bring more?" said Holena fretfully. "You must have eaten them on your way back, you wicked girl."

"No, I have not even tasted them," declared Marushka. "I shook the tree twice. One apple

fell each time. I was not allowed to shake it again, but was told to return home."

Holena would not believe her, and spoke so harshly that Marushka wept bitterly and took refuge in the kitchen.

Holena and her mother ate the apples. Never before had they tasted such delicious fruit. When they had finished the two apples, they both longed for more.

"Mother," said Holena, "give me my cloak, and I will go fetch more apples. I will not send Marushka because the good-for-nothing wretch would eat them on her way. I will find the tree, and no matter who cries 'Stop!' I shall not leave until I have shaken all the apples from the tree."

Holena's mother brought a warm cloak and hood and helped her daughter put them on. Then Holena took the road to the mountain while her mother stood at the window and watched her disappear in the distance.

Snow covered everything, and not a footprint was to be seen anywhere, but Holena pushed on until she reached the mountaintop. There she found the flaming fire and the twelve months seated around it. At first Holena was frightened, and she hesitated to go nearer. But then she went close and warmed her hands without asking permission. The great January inquired severely, "What has brought you here? What do you seek?"

"I need not tell you," replied Holena. "What business is it of yours?"

January frowned and waved his wand over his head. Instantly the sky filled with clouds, snow began to fall, and the fire and the twelve months disappeared. Holena found herself alone in a wild storm. Although she tried to make her way home, she only wandered vainly hither and thither through the white forest.

Meanwhile, Holena's mother looked from the cottage window for her return. The hours passed slowly, and she became alarmed. "Can it be that the apples have charmed her away from home?" she wondered. Finally, she put on her own hood and cloak and set out to search for her daughter. But the snow continued to blow in great drifts, covering everything. The icy north wind whistled through the mountain forests. No voice answered her cry. Neither mother nor daughter ever returned home.

Marushka lived on in the little cottage, which became hers along with the cow and the field. In time an honest young farmer came to share them with her, and they were contented and happy as long as they lived.

# Kuratko the Terrible

# Kuratko the Terrible

THERE WAS ONCE an old couple who had no children.

"If only we had a chick or a child of our own!" Grandmother used to say. "Think how we could pet it and take care of it!"

But Grandfather always answered, "Not at all. We are very well off as we are."

At last the old black hen in the barnyard hatched out a chick. Grandmother was delighted. "See,

Grandpa," she said, "now we have a chick of our own!"

But Grandfather shook his head doubtfully. "I don't like the looks of that chick. There's something strange about it."

But Grandmother wouldn't listen. To her the chick seemed everything it should be. She called it Kuratko and petted it and pampered it as though it were an only child.

Kuratko grew and grew, and soon he developed a huge appetite.

"*Cockadoodledoo!*" he shouted at all hours of the day. "I'm hungry! Give me something to eat!"

"You mustn't feed that chick so much!" Grandfather grumbled. "He's eating us out of house and home."

But Grandmother wouldn't listen. She fed Kuratko and fed him until, sure enough, there came a day when there was nothing left for herself and the old man.

That was a nice how-do-you-do! Grandmother sat working at her spinning wheel trying to forget that she was hungry, and Grandfather sat on his stool nearby too cross to speak to her.

And then, quite as though nothing were the matter, Kuratko strutted into the room, flapped his wings, and crowed, "*Cockadoodledoo!* I'm hungry! Give me something to eat!"

"Not another blessed thing will I ever feed you, you greedy chick!" Grandfather shouted.

"*Cockadoodledoo!*" Kuratko answered. "Then I'll just eat you!"

With that he made one peck at Grandfather and swallowed him down, stool and all!

"Oh, Kuratko!" Grandmother cried. "Where's Grandpa?"

"*Cockadoodledoo!*" Kuratko remarked. "I'm still hungry. I think I'll eat you!" And with that he made one peck at Grandmother and swallowed her down, spinning wheel and all.

Then that terrible chick went strutting down the road, crowing merrily!

He met a washerwoman at work over her washtub.

"Good gracious, Kuratko!" the woman cried. "What a great big crop you've got!"

"*Cockadoodledoo!*" Kuratko said. "I should think my crop was big, for haven't I just eaten Grandmother, spinning wheel and all, and Grandfather, stool and all? But I'm still hungry, so now I'm going to eat you!"

Before the poor woman knew what was happening, Kuratko made one peck at her and swallowed her down, washtub and all!

Then he strutted on down the road, crowing merrily.

Presently he came to a company of soldiers.

"Good gracious, Kuratko!" the soldiers cried. "What a great big crop you've got!"

"*Cockadoodledoo!*" Kuratko replied. "I should

think my crop was big, for haven't I just eaten a washerwoman, tub and all, Grandmother, spinning wheel and all, and Grandfather, stool and all? But I'm still hungry, so now I'm going to eat you!"

Before the soldiers knew what was happening, Kuratko pecked at them and swallowed them down, bayonets and all, one after another, like so many grains of wheat!

Then that terrible chick went on strutting down the road, crowing merrily.

Soon he met Kotsor the cat. Kotsor the cat blinked his eyes and worked his whiskers in surprise.

"Good gracious, Kuratko, what a great big crop you've got!"

"*Cockadoodledoo!*" Kuratko said. "I should think my crop was big, for haven't I just eaten a company of soldiers, bayonets and all, a washerwoman, tub and all, Grandmother, spinning wheel and all, and Grandfather, stool and all? But I'm still hungry, so now I'm going to eat you!"

Before Kotsor the cat knew what was happening, Kuratko made one peck at him and swallowed him down.

But Kotsor the cat was not one to submit tamely to such an indignity. The moment he found himself inside Kuratko, he unsheathed his claws and began to scratch and to tear. He worked until he had torn a great hole in Kuratko's crop. Then Kuratko the terrible chick, when he tried again to crow, toppled over dead!

Kotsor the cat jumped out of Kuratko's crop; after him the company of soldiers marched out; and after them the washerwoman with her tub, Grandmother with her spinning wheel, and Grandfather with his stool. And they all went about their business.

Kotsor the cat followed Grandmother and

Grandfather home and begged them to give him Kuratko for his dinner.

"You may have him for all of me," Grandfather said. "But ask Grandmother. He was her little pet, not mine."

"Indeed, you may have him," Grandmother said. "I see now Grandfather was right. Kuratko was certainly an ungrateful chick, and I never want to hear his name again."

So Kotsor the cat had a wonderful dinner, and to this day when he remembers it he licks his chops and combs his whiskers.

# The Wood Fairy

# The Wood Fairy

ONCE UPON A TIME there was a little girl named Betushka. She lived with her mother, a poor widow who had only a tumbledown cottage and two goats. But in spite of this poverty, Betushka was always merry.

From spring to autumn Betushka drove the goats each day to pasture in a birch wood. Every morning her mother put a slice of bread and an empty spindle into her bag. The spindle would hold the flaxen thread she would spin while she watched the goats. She was too poor to own a distaff on which to wind the flax, so she wound it around her head, and carried it that way to the wood.

"Work hard, Betushka," her mother always said, "and fill the spindle before you return home."

Off skipped Betushka, singing along the way. She danced behind the goats into the wood of birch trees and sat down under a tree. With her left hand she pulled fibers from the flax around her head and with her right hand twirled her spindle so that it hummed over the ground. All the time she sang merrily, and the goats nibbled the green grass among the trees.

When the sun showed that it was midday, Betushka stopped her spinning. She gave each of the goats a morsel of bread and picked a few strawberries to eat with what remained. After this, she sprang up and danced. The sun shone even more warmly and the birds sang yet more sweetly.

After her dance, Betushka began again to spin busily. At evening when she drove the goats home she was able to hand her mother a spindle full of flaxen thread.

One fine spring day, when Betushka was ready as usual to dance, there suddenly appeared before her a most beautiful maiden. The maiden wore a white dress that floated about her as thin as gossamer, and she had golden hair that flowed to her waist and a wreath of forest blossoms upon her head. Betushka was struck silent.

The wood fairy smiled at her and asked in a sweet voice, "Betushka, do you like to dance?"

At this, Betushka lost her fear. "Oh! I could dance all the day long!"

"Come then, let us dance together. I will teach you." She took Betushka and began to dance with her.

Round and round they circled, while sweet music sounded over their heads. The maiden had called upon the birds sitting in the birch trees to accompany them. Nightingales, larks, goldfinches, thrushes, and a clever mocking-bird sang such sweet melodies that Betushka's heart filled with delight. She quite forgot her goats and her spinning. On and on she danced, with feet never weary, till evening when the last rosy rays of sunset were disappearing. The music ceased, and the maiden vanished as suddenly as she had come.

Betushka looked around. There was her spindle—only half filled with thread. Sadly she put it into her bag and drove the goats from the wood. She did not sing while going down the road this time, but reproached herself for forgetting her duty. She resolved she would not do this again. When she reached home she was so quiet that her mother asked if she were ill.

"No, Mother, I am not ill." But she did not tell her mother about the lovely maiden. She hid the half-filled spindle, promising herself to work twice as hard tomorrow to make up for today.

Early the next morning Betushka again drove the goats to pasture, singing merrily as usual. She entered the wood and began her spinning, intending to do twice her usual amount of work.

At noon Betushka picked a few strawberries, but she did not dance. To her goats she said, "Today, I dare not dance. Why don't *you* dance, my little goats?"

"Come and dance with me," called a voice. It was the beautiful maiden.

But this time Betushka was afraid, and she was also ashamed. She asked the maiden to leave her alone. "Before sunset, I must finish my spinning," she said.

The maiden answered, "If you will dance with

me, someone will help you finish your spinning." With the birds singing beautifully, as before, Betushka could not resist. She and the maiden began to dance, and again they danced till evening.

Now when Betushka looked at her nearly empty spindle, she burst into tears. But the maiden unwound the flax from Betushka's head, twined it around a slender birch tree, seized the spindle, and began to spin. The spindle hummed over the ground and grew thick with thread. By the time the sun had dropped from sight, all the flax was spun. As the maiden handed the full spindle to Betushka, she said, "Wind it and grumble not. Remember, wind it and grumble not." Then, suddenly, she disappeared.

Betushka, happy now, drove the goats home, singing as she went, and gave her mother the full spindle. Betushka's mother, however, was not pleased with what Betushka had failed to do the day before and asked her about it. Betushka told her that she had danced, but she kept the maiden a secret.

The next day Betushka went still earlier to the birch wood. The goats grazed while she sang and spun, until at noon the beautiful maiden appeared and again seized Betushka by the waist to dance. While the birds sang for them, the two danced on and on, Betushka quite forgetting her spindle and the goats.

When the sun was setting, Betushka looked around. There was the half-filled spindle! But the maiden grasped Betushka's bag, became invisible for a moment, then handed back the bag stuffed with something light. She ordered her not to look into it before reaching home, and with these words she disappeared.

Betushka started home, not daring to look into the bag. But halfway there she was unable to resist peeking, for the bag was so light she feared a trick. She looked into the bag, and began to weep. It was full of dry birch leaves! Angrily, she tossed some of these out of the bag, but suddenly she stopped—she knew they would make good litter for the goats to sleep on.

Now she was almost afraid to go home. There her mother was awaiting her. "What kind of spindle did you bring me yesterday?" she asked. "I wound and I wound, but the spindle remained full. I grumbled, 'Some evil spirit has spun you,' and at that instant the thread vanished from the spindle. What does this mean?"

Betushka then told her mother about the maiden and their dancing. "That was a wood fairy!" exclaimed her mother, alarmed. "The wood fairies dance at midday and at midnight. If you had been a little boy, you might not have escaped alive. But to little girls the wood fairies often give rich presents." Next she added, "To think that you did not tell me. If I had not

grumbled I might have had a room full of thread."

Betushka then thought of her bag and wondered if there might not, after all, be something under those leaves. She lifted out the spindle and the unspun flax. "Look, Mother!" Her mother looked and clapped her hands. Under the spindle the birch leaves had turned to gold!

Betushka told her mother how the wood fairy had directed her not to peep into her bag until she got home, but that she had not obeyed and had thrown out some of the leaves. "'Tis fortunate you did not empty out the whole bagful," said her mother.

The next morning Betushka and her mother went to the wood to look carefully over the ground where Betushka had thrown out the dry leaves. Only fresh birch leaves lay there, but the gold that Betushka did bring home was enough for a farm with a garden and some cows. She wore beautiful dresses and no longer had to graze the goats. Nothing, however, gave her such delight as she had had dancing with the wood fairy. Often she ran to the birch wood, hoping to see the beautiful maiden, but never again did the wood fairy appear.

# The Shepherd's Nosegay

# The Shepherd's Nosegay

THERE WAS ONCE a King who had a beautiful daughter. When it was time for her to choose a husband, the King set a day and invited all the neighboring Princes to come and see her.

One of these Princes decided that he would like to have a look at the Princess before the

53

others. So he dressed himself in a shepherd's costume: a broad-brimmed hat, a smock, a green vest, tight green breeches to the knees, thick woolen stockings, and sandals. Thus disguised, he set out for the kingdom where the Princess lived. All he took with him were four loaves of bread to eat on the way.

He hadn't gone far when he met a beggar who begged him, in God's name, for a piece of bread. The Prince at once gave him one of the four loaves. A little farther on, a second beggar held out his hand and begged for a piece of bread. To him the Prince gave the second loaf. To a third beggar he gave the third loaf, and to a fourth beggar the last loaf.

The fourth beggar said to him, "Prince in shepherd's guise, your charity will not go unrewarded. Here are four gifts for you, one for each of the loaves of bread that you have given away this day. Take this whip, which has the power of killing anyone it strikes, however gentle the blow. Take this beggar's wallet. It has in it some bread and cheese, but not common bread and cheese, for no matter how much of it you eat, there will always be some left. Take this shepherd's ax. If ever you have to leave your sheep alone, plant it in the earth and the sheep, instead of straying, will graze around it. Last, here is a shepherd's pipe. When you blow upon it your sheep will dance and play. Farewell, and good luck go with you."

The Prince thanked the beggar for his gifts and then trudged on to the kingdom where the beautiful Princess lived. He presented himself at the palace as a shepherd in quest of work, and he told them his name was Yan. The King liked his appearance, and so the next day he was put in charge of a flock of sheep which he drove up the mountainside to pasture.

He planted his shepherd's ax in the midst of

a meadow and, leaving his sheep to graze about it, he went off into the forest hunting adventures. There he came upon a castle where a giant was busy cooking his dinner in a big saucepan.

"Good day to you," Yan said politely.

The giant, who was a rude, unmannerly fellow, bellowed out, "It won't take me long to finish you, you young whippersnapper!"

He raised a great iron club to strike Yan, but Yan, quick as thought, flicked the giant with his whip, and the huge fellow toppled over dead.

The next day he returned to the castle, and there he found another giant in possession.

"Ho, ho!" he roared at sight of Yan. "What, you young whippersnapper, back again! You killed my brother yesterday and now I'll kill you."

He raised his great iron club to strike Yan, but Yan skipped nimbly aside. Then he flicked the giant with his whip, and the huge fellow toppled over dead.

When Yan returned to the castle the third day, there were no more giants about. So he wandered from room to room to see what treasures were there.

In one room he found a big chest. He struck it smartly, and immediately two burly men jumped out and, bowing low before him, asked, "What does the master of the castle desire?"

"Show me everything there is to be seen," Yan ordered.

So the two servants of the chest showed him everything—jewels and treasures and gold. Then they led him out into the gardens, where the most wonderful flowers in the world were blooming. Yan plucked some of these and made them into a nosegay.

That afternoon, as he drove his sheep home, he played on his magic pipe, and the sheep, pairing off two by two, began to dance and frisk about him. All the people in the village ran out to see the strange sight and clapped their hands for joy.

The Princess ran to the palace window, and when she saw the sheep dancing two by two, she also laughed and clapped her hands. Then the wind whiffed her a smell of the wonderful nosegay that Yan was carrying, and she said to her serving maid, "Run down to the shepherd and tell him the Princess desires his nosegay."

The serving maid delivered the message to Yan, but he shook his head and said, "Tell your mistress that whoever wants this nosegay must come herself and say, 'Yanitchko, give me that nosegay.'"

When the Princess heard this, she laughed and said, "What an odd shepherd! I see I must go myself."

So the Princess herself came out to Yan and said, "Yanitchko, give me that nosegay."

But Yan smiled and shook his head. "Whoever

wants this nosegay must say, 'Yanitchko, please give me that nosegay.'"

The Princess was a merry girl, so she laughed and said, "Yanitchko, please give me that nosegay."

Yan gave it to her at once, and she thanked him sweetly.

The next day Yan went again to the castle garden and plucked another nosegay. Then in the afternoon he drove his sheep through the village as before, playing his pipe. The Princess was standing at the palace window waiting to see him. When the wind brought her a whiff of the fresh nosegay that was even more fragrant than the first one, she ran out to Yan and said, "Yanitchko, please give me that nosegay."

But Yan smiled and shook his head. "Whoever wants this nosegay must say, 'My dear Yanitchko, I beg you most politely please to give me that nosegay.'"

"My dear Yanitchko," the Princess repeated demurely, "I beg you most politely please to give me that nosegay."

So Yan gave her the second nosegay. The Princess put it in her window, and the fragrance filled the village until people from far and near came to see it.

After that, every day Yan gathered a nosegay for the Princess, and every day the Princess stood at the palace window waiting to see the handsome shepherd. And always when she asked for the nosegay, she said, "Please."

In this way a month went by, and the day arrived when the neighboring Princes were to come to meet the Princess. They were to come in fine array, the people said, and the Princess had ready a kerchief and a ring for the one who would please her most.

Yan planted the ax in the meadow and, leaving the sheep to graze about it, went to the castle, where he ordered the servants of the chest to dress him as befitted his rank. They put a red suit upon him and gave him a sorrel horse with trappings of silver.

So he rode to the palace and took his place with the other Princes, but behind them, so that the Princess had to crane her neck to see him.

One by one the various Princes rode by the Princess, but to none of them did the Princess give her kerchief and ring. Yan was the last to salute her, and instantly she handed him her favors.

Then, before the King or the other suitors could speak to him, Yan put spurs to his horse and rode off.

That evening, as usual, when he was driving home his sheep, the Princess ran out to him and said, "Yan, it was you!"

But Yan laughed and put her off. "How can a poor shepherd be a Prince?" he asked.

The Princess was not convinced, and she said that in another month, when the Princes were to come again, she would find out.

So for another month Yan tended sheep and plucked nosegays for the merry little Princess, and the Princess waited for him at the palace window every afternoon, and when she saw him she always spoke to him politely and said, "Please."

When the day for the second meeting of the Princes came, the servants of the chest arrayed Yan in a suit of white and gave him a white horse with trappings of red. Yan again rode to the palace and took his place with the other Princes, but behind them, so that the Princess had to crane her neck to see him.

Again the suitors rode by the Princess one by one, but at each of them she shook her head impatiently and kept her kerchief and ring until Yan saluted her.

As soon as the ceremony was over, Yan put spurs to his horse and rode off. Although the King sent after him to bring him back, Yan was able to escape.

That evening when he was driving home his sheep, the Princess ran out to him and said, "Yanitchko, it was you! I know it was!"

But again Yan laughed and put her off and asked her how she could think such a thing of a poor shepherd.

Again the Princess was not convinced, and she said in another month, when the Princes were to come for the third and last time, she would make sure.

So for another month Yan tended his sheep and plucked nosegays for the merry little Princess, and the Princess waited for him at the palace window every afternoon, and when she saw him she always said politely, "Please."

For the third meeting of the Princes the

servants of the chest arrayed Yan in a gorgeous suit of black and gave him a black horse with golden trappings studded in diamonds. He rode to the palace and took his place behind the other suitors. Things went as before, and again the Princess saved her kerchief and ring for him.

This time when he tried to ride off, the other suitors surrounded him, and before he escaped, one of them wounded him on the foot.

He galloped back to the castle in the forest, changed once again into his shepherd's clothes, and returned to the meadow where his sheep were grazing. There he sat down and bound up his wounded foot in the kerchief which the Princess had given him. Then, when he had eaten some bread and cheese from his magic wallet, he stretched himself out in the sun and fell asleep.

Meanwhile the Princess, who was sorely vexed that her mysterious suitor had again escaped, slipped out of the palace and ran up the mountain path to see for herself whether the shepherd was really with his sheep. She found Yan asleep and, when she saw her kerchief bound about his foot, she knew that he was the Prince.

She woke him up and cried, "You are he! You know you are!"

Yan looked at her and laughed and asked, "How can I be a Prince?"

"But I know you are!" the Princess said. "Oh Yanitchko, dear Yanitchko, I beg you please to tell me!"

So then Yan, because he always did anything the Princess asked him when she said "Please," told her his true name and his rank.

The Princess, overjoyed to hear that her dear shepherd was really a Prince, brought him back to her father, the King.

"This is the man I shall marry," she said. "This and none other."

So Yan and the merry Princess were married and lived very happily. And the people of the country always say when they speak of the Princess, "That's a Princess for you! Why, even if she *is* a Princess, she always says 'Please' to her own husband!"

# The Three Golden Hairs of Grandfather Know All

# The Three Golden Hairs of Grandfather Know All

ONCE THERE LIVED a King who loved to hunt wild beasts in his forest. One day while chasing a deer he lost his way. He wandered about alone until, just as it was growing dark, he came to a charcoal-burner's small thatched cottage.

"Will you show me the way to the high road?" the King asked. "I will give you good money if you will get me out of the forest."

The man answered, "I would go with you gladly, but I cannot leave my wife. Will you not pass the night under our roof? There is sweet hay in the loft where you may rest. In the morning I will be your guide."

That night a son was born to the charcoal-burner and his wife.

The King lay on the hay in the loft and could not sleep. About midnight, he looked through a crack in the floor into the room below. He saw the charcoal-burner and his wife asleep, and near the newly born babe were three old women dressed in white, each holding a lighted taper, talking together.

The first said, "On this boy I bestow the gift of meeting great dangers."

The second said, "I bestow on him the power

to escape all these dangers and live to an old age."

The third added, "I bestow upon him as wife the Princess born at the same hour, who is daughter of the King sleeping up there in the loft."

Thereupon the three old women snuffed out their tapers, and all was quiet.

To the King, these words were like a sword piercing his chest. He knew that these women were the Fates. All night he lay awake trying to think how he could prevent the words of the third Fate from coming true.

At daybreak the baby began to cry. The charcoal-burner rose up and saw, alas, that his wife was no longer living.

"My child is an orphan!" he cried. "What will become of him without a mother's care?"

"Give me the child," said the King. "I will see that he is always happy, and I will give you

money so that you shall not need to burn char-
coal for a living."

The poor man was relieved. He gladly accepted the King's promise to send someone for
the child.

When the King came to his castle, his people
announced with great joy that a beautiful daughter had been born to him. She was born the very
night that he had seen the three Fates.

Instead of looking pleased, the King's face
grew dark. He directed one of his servants to go
to the charcoal-burner's cottage. "Hand the
man this money, and he will give you a little
child. You must take the child, and on your way
home drown it in the river. If you don't, you
shall come to this end yourself."

The servant found the cottage in the forest.
The charcoal-burner lay the child in a basket
and gave it to him. The man traveled on till he
came to a place where the river was deep, and

there he threw the basket into the water. When the King heard the servant's story, he answered only, "Good-bye, unbidden son-in-law."

The King naturally thought that the child was dead. But it was not so. The basket floated on the water, and in it the child slept as peacefully as if in a cradle with his mother by him singing lullabies.

Now it happened that the basket drifted near a fisherman's hut. The fisherman was sitting on the bank, mending his net, when he noticed something floating on the water. He sprang into his boat and rowed after it. When he caught up the basket, he found the child, and at once ran to tell his wife the good news. "Look, you have always wished for a son. Here is a beautiful little boy the river has brought us."

The fisherman's wife cried with joy. She took the child and loved it as her own. She and her husband named him Plavachek, which means

Floater—because he had floated to them on the river.

The river flowed on and the years, too, while Plavachek grew into a handsome youth. Far and wide, his equal could not be found.

One hot summer day the King, riding on horseback and alone, chanced to pass the fisherman's hut. He stopped and asked the fisherman for a drink of water. When Plavachek brought it, the King looked at the lad closely.

"A splendid young man you have here. Is he your son?"

"He is and he isn't," answered the fisherman. "Just twenty years ago I caught him in a basket floating down the river. My wife and I brought him up as our own son."

The world grew dark before the King's eyes. He knew that this was the boy he had told his servingman to drown. Quickly he sprang from his horse and said, "I need a messenger to carry a letter to my castle. Could this young man go?"

"Only command and he shall go," replied the fisherman.

The King sat down and wrote a letter to his Queen, saying, "Let this young man I send to you be pierced with a sword. He is my dangerous enemy. Let it be done before my return. Such is my will." He folded the letter and sealed it with the royal seal.

On his way Plavachek had to go through a forest so dense that he lost the path. It began to grow dark before his journey was nearly over. But then he met an old woman who asked, "Where are you going, Plavachek? Where are you going?"

"I am bearing this letter from the King to the Queen, but I have lost my way. Could you put me on the right road?"

"You could not reach the castle tonight," said the old woman. "Stay with me in my cottage. You will not be with strangers, for I am your god-mother."

Plavachek agreed. They had taken only a few steps when a cottage appeared before them. While Plavachek slept, the old woman took the letter from his pocket and in its place put another written in the same hand and sealed with the same seal. But this one read, "Have this young man I send to you married to our daughter at once. I have chosen him as my son-in-law. Let the marriage take place before my return. Such is my pleasure."

When the Queen received the letter, she was surprised. But at once she ordered preparations to be made for the wedding. Both she and her daughter admired Plavachek, and Plavachek was equally pleased with his bride.

After some days the King came home. When he learned what had taken place, he was very angry with the Queen.

"But you bade me have the wedding before your return. Come, read your letter again. Here it is."

The King examined the letter. The writing, the paper, and the seal were all clearly his own. He called his son-in-law and asked what had happened to him on his journey and where he had stopped. Plavachek hid nothing. He told the King how he had lost his way and had spent the night in an old woman's cottage in the forest.

"What was she like?" asked the King.

The King knew that the old woman was the same one who twenty years before had foretold that his daughter would marry the charcoal-burner's son. After thinking and thinking, he said, "What is done is done, but you are not to be my son-in-law so easily. If you wish to keep your wife, you must bring us a present of three golden hairs from the head of Grandfather Know All."

In this way the King thought he would get rid of his humble son-in-law.

Plavachek took leave of his wife and set off. "I know not which way to go," he said to himself, but since Fate was his godmother, he found it easy to take the right road. He traveled long and far, over mountains, through valleys and across rivers, until he reached the shores of the Black Sea. There he saw a boat and in it a ferryman.

"May God bless you, old ferryman," he called.

"You, also, traveler. Where are you going?"

"To Grandfather Know All's castle for three of his golden hairs."

"Ah, then you are very welcome," cried the ferryman. "For a weary time I have been waiting for such a messenger as you. For twenty years have I ferried people across, and not one has helped me. If you will promise to ask Grandfather Know All when I shall be released from my labor, I will ferry you over."

Plavachek promised, and the old man ferried him to the opposite bank. He continued his journey on foot until he came to a town half in ruins.

A funeral procession was passing, and a man was following his father's coffin with tears running down his cheeks.

"May God comfort you in your distress," said Plavachek.

"Thank you, good traveler. Where are you going?"

"To the castle of Grandfather Know All for three of his golden hairs."

"To the castle of Grandfather Know All, indeed! What a pity you did not come sooner. We have been expecting such a messenger as you. I will take you to my master the King."

When Plavachek presented himself at court, the King said to him, "We hear that you are on your way to see Grandfather Know All. We have here a tree which once bore the Apples of Youth. If a man ate one of those apples, even though he were dying, he would be cured and become young again. But for the last twenty years the tree has borne no fruit. Will you ask Grandfather Know All what is the cause of this? I will reward you richly."

Plavachek promised to ask the question, and the King sent him on his way with good wishes. On his journey Plavachek came to a large and beautiful city where all was sad and silent. Near the city gate, he met an old man leaning on a stick and walking with difficulty.

"May God bless you, good old man," said Plavachek.

"And you, too, my handsome young traveler. And where do you go?"

"To the castle of Grandfather Know All for three of his golden hairs."

"What a pity you did not come sooner. We have been expecting such a messenger as you. I will take you to my master the King."

When they came into the King's presence, the King said, "I hear that you are going to see Grandfather Know All. We once had here a spring out of which flowed the Water of Life. When a man drank of it, even if he were dying, straightaway he became well. If a man were dead, and they sprinkled his body with the water, he rose up and walked. For twenty years now the water has ceased to flow. Will you ask Grandfather Know All how the water may be restored? I will reward you richly."

Plavachek promised to ask this question, and the King sent him on with good wishes. He traveled through deep dark forests in the midst of which he found a green meadow. Beautiful flowers grew here, and in the center of the meadow stood a golden castle so brilliant with light that it seemed to be built of fire. It was the castle of Grandfather Know All.

Plavachek entered the castle but found no one there except an old woman who sat in a corner spinning.

"Greetings, Plavachek. I am glad that you have come."

She was his godmother, the woman who had given him shelter in her cottage when he was carrying the King's letter.

"What brings you here from so far?"

"The King would not have me for his son-in-law for nothing. He has sent me to Grandfather Know All to get three golden hairs."

The woman laughed. "Grandfather Know All is, my child, the shining sun himself. In the morning he is a boy, at midday a man, and in the evening an old grandfather. I am not your godmother for nothing. I will see that you have three hairs from his head. But you cannot remain here. My son is a good lad, but when he comes home he is hungry, and would likely order you to be roasted for his supper. I will turn this empty bucket upside down, and you shall hide in it."

Plavachek begged his godmother to get from Grandfather Know All answers to the three questions he had been asked.

"I will do so, and you must listen to what he says."

Suddenly a blast of wind howled round the castle and the Sun entered by a western window. He was an old man with golden hair.

"I smell man's flesh," said he. "You have someone here, Mother."

"Star of the day, whom could I have here that you would not see sooner than I? You fly all day over the world and get the scent of man's flesh. It is no wonder that when you come home at evening it clings to you still."

Grandfather Know All said nothing, but sat down to his supper. When she saw that he was sleeping, she pulled out a hair and threw it on the ground. It fell with the sound a guitar makes when touched by skillful fingers.

"What do you want, Mother?" asked he.

"Nothing, my son, nothing. I was sleeping and had a strange dream."

"What was it, Mother?"

"I thought I was in a place where there was a well, fed by a spring, with water which cured all diseases. Even a dying man if he drank of it became well straightaway. If a dead man was sprinkled with the water, he came to life again. But for twenty years the well has run dry. What must be done to make it flow again?"

"That is very simple. A frog has lodged itself in the opening of the spring. If the frog is killed, the water will flow again."

Grandfather Know All fell asleep again, and his mother pulled out a second golden hair and threw it on the ground.

"What do you want, Mother?"

"Nothing, my son, nothing. I was sleeping, and I had a strange dream. I saw a large town where there grew an apple tree. The tree used to bear fruit that could make an old man young again. But for twenty years the tree has not borne fruit. What can be done to make it fruitful once more?"

"This is not difficult. Among the roots of the tree there hides a snake. You must kill the snake and plant the tree in another place, then it will bear fruit as before."

Grandfather Know All fell asleep again, and the woman pulled out the third golden hair.

"What is it, Mother, that you will not let me sleep?" cried he, ready to get up.

"Lie down, my son, lie down. I am sorry I awoke you, but I have had a strange dream. I dreamed I saw an old ferryman on the shores of the Black Sea. He complained that for twenty years he had gone back and forth over the sea and no one had come to take his place. How much longer must he go on rowing?"

"He is a stupid fellow! He has but to place the oars in the hands of the first comer and jump ashore. Whoever receives the oars will replace him as ferryman. But let me sleep. I must rise early, for I must dry the tears of a Princess. She spends all night weeping for her husband, who has been sent by her father to get three of my golden hairs."

Next morning a wind rose up outside. Instead of an old man, a beautiful child with golden hair sprang up. He bade his mother good-bye and flew out of the eastern window.

The mother lifted the bucket from over Plavachek and said, "Here are the three golden hairs. Now you have heard the answers to your questions. You will not see me again, for you will have no further need of me."

Plavachek thanked the old woman and went on his way. When he came to the city with the dried-up spring, the King inquired what news he brought.

"Good news," said Plavachek. "Clean out the spring, and kill the frog that sits in the opening. The water will flow as before."

The King had this done at once and rejoiced to see the water rush out in a full stream. He gave Plavachek twelve white horses loaded with as much gold and silver as they could carry.

When Plavachek came to the second town, the King there asked what news he brought.

"Good news," cried Plavachek. "Dig up your apple tree, and kill the snake that lives among its roots. Plant the tree in another place, and it will bear apples as before."

The King had this done straightaway. No sooner was it transplanted than it burst into blossoms.

The King rejoiced. He gave Plavachek twelve black horses loaded with as much wealth as they could carry.

Plavachek journeyed to the shores of the Black Sea. There the ferryman asked him if Grandfather Know All had told him when his labor would end.

"Yes," said Plavachek. "Ferry me over and then I will tell you what he said."

The ferryman carried Plavachek and his twenty-four horses over the sea and then Plavachek said, "When you ferry another traveler across, put the oars in his hands as soon as you touch land. He will become ferryman in your place."

The King could not believe his eyes when Plavachek gave him the three golden hairs of Grandfather Know All. As for the Princess, his young wife, she wept for joy.

"But how did you get such beautiful horses and so much wealth?" she asked.

"I earned them," answered Plavachek. "They are payment for the hardships I endured and the services I gave. I helped one King regain the Apples of Youth, apples that make old men young. And I helped another King get back the Water of Life, water that makes weak men strong and brings the dead back to life."

"Apples of Youth! Water of Life!" cried the King. "I will go find these treasures for myself. What joy! I shall become young again, and I shall live forever."

The King wasted no time. That very day he started off to find the Apples of Youth and the

Water of Life, and he has not returned yet, for he journeyed by way of the Black Sea.

The charcoal-burner's son became King, as Fate had decided, and lived happily ever after.

# About This Series

I N RECENT DECADES, folk tales and fairy tales from all corners of the earth have been made available in a variety of handsome collections and in lavishly illustrated picture books. But in the 1950s, such a rich selection was not yet available. The classic fairy and folk tales were most often found in cumbersome books with small print and few illustrations. Helen Jones, then children's book editor at Little, Brown and Company, accepted a proposal from a Boston librarian for an ambitious series with a simple goal — to put an international selection of stories into the hands of children. The tales would be published in slim volumes, with wide margins and ample leading, and illustrated by a cast of contemporary artists. The result was a unique series of books intended for children to read by themselves — the Favorite Fairy Tales series. Available only in hardcover for many years, the books have now been reissued in paperbacks that feature new illustrations and covers.

The series embraces the stories of sixteen different

countries: France, England, Germany, India, Ireland, Sweden, Poland, Russia, Spain, Czechoslovakia, Scotland, Greece, Japan, Denmark, Italy, and Norway. Some of these stories may seem violent or fantastical to our modern sensibilities, yet they often reflect the deepest yearnings and imaginings of the human mind and heart.

Virginia Haviland traveled abroad frequently and was able to draw upon librarians, storytellers, and writers in countries as far away as Japan to help make her selections. But she was also an avid researcher with a keen interest in rare books, and most of the stories she included in the series were found through a diligent search of old collections. Ms. Haviland was associated with the Boston Public Library for nearly thirty years — as a children's and branch librarian, and eventually as Readers Advisor to Children. She reviewed for *The Horn Book Magazine* for almost thirty years and in 1963 was named Head of the Children's Book Section of the Library of Congress. Ms. Haviland remained with the Library of Congress for nearly twenty years and wrote and lectured about children's literature throughout her career. She died in 1988.